ROCKY
&
PENELOPE

The Perfect Exchange

Fairy Tales Really Do
Come True—If Only
You Believe

ROCKY & PENELOPE

The Perfect Exchange

Story by Charlie Em

Illustrations by Taralee Tilma

AHELIA
PUBLISHING

Written
just for you,
darling.

Once upon a time, in a land not as far away as you might think, there lived a boy. He was a sweet boy, to be sure, but there was one little problem—he only had one leg! Now, this wouldn't be a problem for most little boys because most little boys would just adapt and be content to hobble along or make due. Most little boys would say, "Well, this is what I've been given, so this is all I get."

WEST
EAST

But not Rocky. Oh no, never!

Now, Rocky wasn't particularly unsatisfied with his one leg, and he was not angry or impatient about the whole predicament. But you see, there was something different about Rocky. Way down deep, in a place most boys and girls never visit, Rocky understood that he was meant for much more than hobbling along on one leg. In fact, he wasn't sure that even two legs would be enough to carry him to where he wanted to go or be sufficient for how fast he wanted to run.

As the years passed quickly, like clicks on a camera, Rocky grew up. Sometimes, he grew by leaps and bounds, barely recognizing himself when he looked in the mirror. His chubby baby face began taking on the shape of a man; his skin turned rough and a few deep lines and even some scars began appearing here and there. Oh, how he disliked those lines. To Rocky, they were signs of too many clicks on the camera of a life with only one leg.

Sometimes, at least to him, it seemed he grew oh-so-slowly. Rocky found himself beginning to wonder why he'd ever dreamed so big, or thought he could have more than his fair share of legs. He'd wonder if somehow, even with only one leg, he might still be able to climb the highest mountains or swim the deepest seas.

Rocky sometimes became discouraged with the answers that would try to plant themselves into the soil of his heart. Nevertheless, and sometimes more than others, but all the time a little bit, that place so deep down inside of him — that place most people never even dare to consider let alone dream about — kept right on tugging at that boy who'd turned into a man.

Rocky didn't know how, or why, or where it came from, but he just knew that his life was about to change. That place so deep down was telling him — whispering at first — that he was about to get so many legs he'd barely be able to keep up to his dreams, and Rocky's dreams were huge indeed.

Now, let it be known that a long ways away in a land where pigs could fly and unicorns danced on rainbows, there was a sweet little girl who had a bunch of extra legs. She never knew why, when most people were given only two legs, she had so many more.

Penelope was always confused by such a thing and often, it was quite a conundrum. After all, this little girl thought and pondered and wondered all the time and she liked to understand the reasons behind such things as extra legs!

One day Penelope was talking to Queen Charlotte, the one who ran the castle — of course — and she was asking Queen Charlotte if she ever noticed that Penelope had too many legs.

"Well, most certainly, Penelope, you do NOT have too many legs!" the Queen laughed. "You are just the keeper of the legs — they don't belong to you, my dear!" Queen Charlotte laughed at such silly thoughts of the young princess.

"Who am I keeping legs for?" Penelope asked, altogether confused and thoroughly tired of keeping the legs.

Queen Charlotte stopped laughing; she was a very wise Queen, after all. She bent right down so she could look straight into Penelope's eyes because after all, Penelope wasn't very big and had too many tears in her eyes to look up to the Queen.

"Oh, dear little Penelope," the Queen whispered and wiped a tear that had forced its way from Penelope's eyes. "There is one who is looking for you —he's looking for what you've been holding for him."

"So I am supposed to give the legs to that one?" Penelope was so very confused in her wonderings, but happy with the idea of getting rid of the legs.

"I suppose. But Penelope" said the Queen, "he's been carrying something for you as well so you won't be giving anything, you'll be making a trade."

Well, of course, Penelope was as confused as ever, even after talking to Queen Charlotte who was, after all, the wisest Queen in all the land. Every day, Penelope would find the Queen and ask one hundred questions and the Queen would smile and always give the same answer. No matter what the question was, the answer was always the same …

"You'll know Penelope … you will know."

Well, as it does, the camera of time clicked by, year after year rolled on, snapshots of life imprinted themselves into the sands of days past. Penelope grew up and while she searched and searched for that one to whom the legs belonged, she could find him nowhere.

Oh sure, a couple of times she thought she had, and a few times people would come along who tricked her into believing that what she held onto for so long belonged to them. But sadly, Penelope was more concerned with finding the one to whom the legs belonged than she was with being wise or making a trade.

More than once, she gave the extra legs away only to remember that it was supposed to be a trade of some sort. Often, the words of Queen Charlotte would come to her and Penelope would remember about the trade.

She would take back the legs since the ones she gave them to had nothing to trade and only wanted to take. Penelope would walk away with her heart broken, her fear deeper, her loneliness a full measure. Finally, she stopped looking for that one for whom she was holding the legs. Her heart had been chipped away, bit-by-bit, for so long that it seemed there wasn't much left of it. So, as any broken-down-leg-carrying-little-girl would, Penelope decided to put her heart in a box, wrap a heavy chain around it, and lock it up tight. She was certain she'd never be willing to unlock the box again, so Penelope headed straight to the sea.

With all her might — which was a very great deal for such a small girl —Penelope threw the key into the sea and watched as it sunk down ... down ... down ... down ... until it was gone.

"There!" she shouted to the wind. "Now my heart will be safe

and sound." And truly, she believed it would be.

Now, all the while Penelope was busy running around with her heart locked up tight, she knew — in some space so deep down that few people ever even dare to visit — that she still had those extra legs! She'd tried and tried to give them away, but never for a trade. Those to whom she gave the legs, only used them until they got tired of playing and then tossed them back at her and ran away.

Penelope still had those extra legs with no one to give them to. So, year after year, with her heart locked up tight and no key to open the chains, she dragged those legs around promising herself she'd never give them away again. "NEVER," she'd tell herself. "NEVER," she'd tell others who asked for those legs. "NEVER," she'd scream to her friends when they told her she wasn't meant to carry the legs forever.

So on and on it went. Oh yes, some came around who asked for the legs, but Penelope would pretend she didn't hear them because most surely they had nothing to trade and only wanted the legs for selfish reasons. She knew they were like the others who would get bored of the legs and throw them back at her. Then they would run away, leaving her to gather the legs once again.

Now, far across the sea, in that land that was so very far — yet not as far as you'd think — away, stood Rocky. He had gone down to the sea to ask the winds if he could have more legs because surely, his dreams were far too big and he wanted to run much too fast to have only one.

Well, things being what they are, and this being a made-up story and all, Rocky thought he saw something glimmering in the sand. He hobbled over on his one leg, but just as he was about to bend over and pick up the glimmering thing, the sea snuck in and grabbed it. Rocky saw, just as the sea gobbled it up, that what had been glimmering in the sand was a beautiful, golden key.

He wondered briefly — which was exactly the same amount of time that he'd seen the key — what kind of a lock a key as beautiful as that one must open.

For days and days — and every day in between — Rocky went down to the sea with his fingers crossed, hoping to find that key. He demanded the sea bring it back. He begged the sea to spit it out. He pleaded with the sea to return it. Day after day — and every day in between.

Then it happened. One day, the last day probably because Rocky was growing tired of going down and pleading with the sea, there it was. Laying in the sand in exactly the same placed he'd seen it the first time, was the key. Rocky wasn't going to lose it again so as quickly as he could, that man — for his boyhood was long behind him by now — grabbed the key.

Oh, it was indeed beautiful. He turned it over in his hands and ever-so-gently brushed off the sand. It glistened ... it shone. Rocky didn't know, of course, what it was for, but he put it on a rope and hung it around his neck. "Surely," he reasoned, "if anyone knows what this key will unlock, they'll see it and tell me straightaway. Certainly a key so beautiful must belong to a lock equally as beautiful!"

Every day Rocky went down to the sea and asked the wind to carry him to the one who held the lock. Every day, the wind took his words across the sea. Every day, Penelope's heart got a little less satisfied with staying locked in the box but, "What can I do?" she'd cry to the Queen. "I've thrown the key into the sea!"

"Well, darling," Queen Charlotte would say to Miss Penelope, a grown woman by now with a very sad heart, "let's go down to the sea and ask the winds to return the key."

So every day, day in and day out — and every day in between — Miss Penelope and Queen Charlotte would journey to the sea and with a loud voice, cry out. "Oh sea, please return to me the key to my heart. It's dreadfully sad and needs to be let out of the box lest it dies altogether." Every day the sea would be silent but the winds would take Penelope's words and carry them across to the other side.

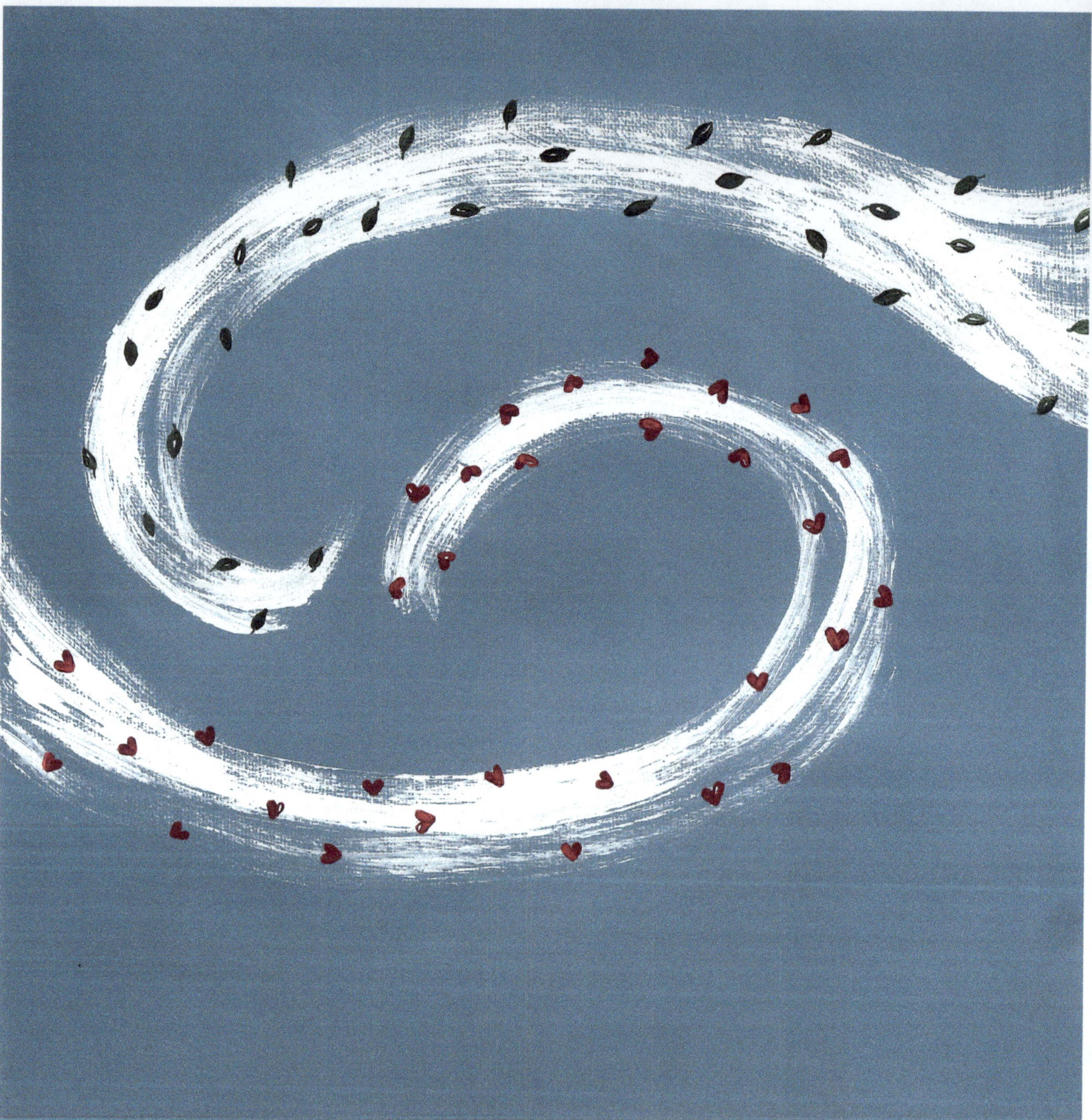

Now, as all good fairytales go, one quite perfectly peaceful day, Rocky's voice — which was being carried on the wings of the wind — accidentally bumped into Miss Penelope's voice which was also being carried by the wind's wings. As the two winds met, they began to dance. One held the key and one held the chains that locked the heart which held the legs.

Really, and fully without Rocky knowing anything of it at all, he held the key to his dreams — the key to the box that chained the heart which held his legs. He held his own key!

As the winds met, they danced and swayed and mingled and wove together. They had a conversation and became the best of friends. The winds decided that since Rocky had held his dreams for so long, and had wondered about the secret place so deep inside that most people never even notice it — and since Miss Penelope had tried so hard to find that one to whom the legs belonged until her heart was too broken to keep on looking — that the winds would intercede and bring all things together.

Those graceful winds decided to bring the key to the heart and the legs to the dreamer and set both free to dance together under the moonlight.

It wasn't very long after the winds made their plan that Rocky decided to build a boat and go out to sea. The boy-turned-man was about ready to give up on his dreams and he decided that dropping those dreams into the middle of the sea was the best place for them. He could forget them there.

"Unretrievable," he muttered to the rain as he paddled out to the sea.

About that same time, Queen Charlotte died. Miss Penelope was so broken up about it because — well — because Queen Charlotte had raised little Penelope and had taught her about everything there was to know. The only thing Penelope could think to do now was to run away.

That little girl, now a grown woman, ran down to the sea and found a boat. Penelope wasn't always one to think things through and more times than not got herself into pickles and often, her shenanigans left her embarrassed. This was probably going to be one of those times, but at the moment, Penelope was fleeing so she never paid any attention to what the outcome might be; she rarely did.

As in all good fairytales, a great storm arose on the sea, but Rocky didn't care. He was determined to get to the middle of the sea and drown his dreams. Dark nights covered the sea but Penelope didn't care. She was determined to get to the middle of the sea and drown her sorrows. On and on it went, Rocky coming one way, Penelope coming the other.

Now, the sea is a very big place and so to think that, just maybe, Rocky and Penelope could somehow meet in the middle seems a bit more than a coincidence, wouldn't you think?

Oh, but the winds — don't forget about the winds. They had danced and intertwined and planned and when winds make a plan, nothing can stop it. So after many days, Miss Penelope reached the middle of the sea. She sat in her stolen boat and cried rivers of tears. It was a very good thing she was in a boat or she may have drowned, her tears were so many in number. But suddenly, they stopped. Not even one more tear fell!

Something had surrounded her. She couldn't see what it was, but she could feel it. There was no doubt that something was in the air and had enveloped her with an odd, but welcome peace — one she'd never felt before. Miss Penelope dried her eyes and looked all around. She searched and strained until finally, something came into her view. It was off in the distance, to be sure, but it was there nonetheless.

The closer this thing in the air came, the warmer the peace felt in her soul — and on her skin. The sunlight passed quickly but as she watched, a boat came into view and as she watched some more, she saw there was a man in the boat. Penelope noticed, as they came close enough to one another, that his eyes caught hers and something magical happened. It was nearly dark by now, but the moon being full and all, decided to help the winds and gave off an extra beam of light — just for tonight — just for this moment in time.

In only one look, before Penelope's heart could thump-thump even one complete beat, it suddenly felt unbroken. There was something in this man's eyes that saw straight into her heart and she couldn't look away. Penelope knew, in one instant, before she knew his name or his story, that he was the one to whom her extra legs belonged.

Penelope couldn't explain it then — and she can't explain it now — but she keeps right on trying nevertheless. Until her breath runs out, that girl-turned-woman, will keep on trying to explain what happened in that moment when the winds blew and the moon shimmered. It was as though the pieces she'd been missing all her life were in that boy-turned-man's boat. All the tears she'd ever cried, that boat was now riding on.

It was as if, somehow, her tears had made a way for the boat — that held the man — who carried the key to her heart — to get to her. No, that must be pure nonsense. Perhaps it was, perhaps it wasn't. Nobody will ever know except the winds and the moon and the stardust in the air.

Somehow, and completely without
any reasonable explanation, that
one in the boat, was her one.

As Rocky's boat got close enough for Penelope to see clearly, she saw it; she saw the key. That boy-turned-man had the key to her heart and she held the legs to his dreams.

"A perfect trade," she heard the wind sing but of course, wind doesn't sing and so it must have been the voice of Queen Charlotte who had continued to watch over Miss Penelope from the wind's embrace.

Perhaps, and this is only a suggestion for it seems rather nonsensical really, Queen Charlotte had become entwined with the winds or perhaps, she just used them as her chariot.

Without knowing how any of it happened, that deep place in Penelope — the place so deep that few dare to travel — met with the deep place in Rocky — the place so deep that most never bother to look for it — and together they danced under the moonlight on the waves of the sea.

To this day, each day, and every day in between, Miss Penelope will try with all her might to explain to Rocky his value (which is deeper than the deepest sea), and his worth (with which there's nothing big enough to measure it).

He doesn't understand it though and he never will completely, but that, you see, has a very reasonable explanation. If the day ever came when Rocky fully understood all of the things which Miss Penelope was trying to explain, she'd have no more reason to explain anything at all.

Besides that, there will never be an end to such things because every day, day after day, and every day in between, Rocky grows deeper and more valuable and far beyond measure in his worth. So you see, there will never be an end to Penelope telling him about such things. Just as she finishes her explaining, a whole new layer of marvelousness explodes and she has to start all over again — not at the beginning, but exactly where she left off.

You see, Rocky is one of a kind. There's none like him in all the earth. He's a ruby, an emerald, a gem of irreplaceable value, and Miss Penelope knows it. She saw it there, on the sea, before he ever touched her ear or kissed her lips. She saw it and it embraced her. The essence of Rocky still embraces Penelope and his kindness heals her heart every day — day in and day out — and every day in between.

So there it was then — that was that. All of the answers to all of the questions sat in that boat in the middle of the sea under the moon.

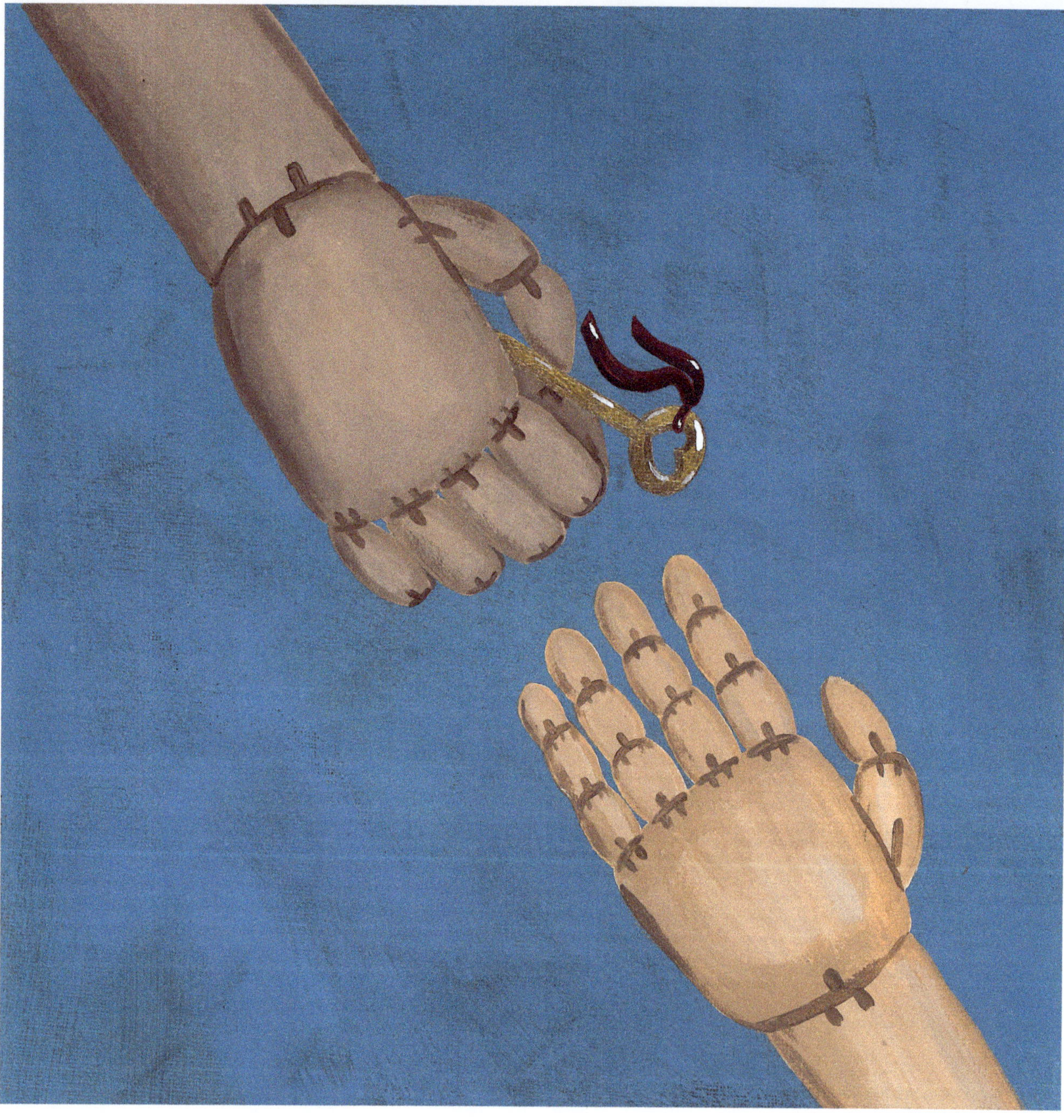

"That's my key," Penelope sang out to this stranger in the boat resting on the sea of her tears.

"What's it for?" he asked, for truly he didn't know.

"It's for my heart, of course. You see, I locked it up so the few pieces I had left wouldn't get lost."

"May I unlock it?" Rocky asked and as he stood up in his boat, Penelope saw that he was missing a leg and so, of course, she replied with the most obvious question. "Only if I can give you the legs I've been holding."

So that was that. The trade was made. A key to a broken heart for the legs of a broken dream. And at that moment, all was right with the world. Both Penelope and Rocky were made whole and their hearts were mended and their dreams were given life and together they danced under a moonlit sky and, of course, they lived happily ever after because after all, it was a perfect trade and that is precisely how all good fairy tales must end.

THE END